Good Night Twinklegator

For Robert,
Dorian,
and Sakura

Library of Congress Cataloging-in-Publication Data

Stone, Kazuko G.
Good Night Twinklegator/by Kazuko G. Stone.
p. cm.
Summary: Aligay plays connect-the-dots with the stars to make
Twinklegator, an imaginary friend, who comes down to earth to play.
ISBN 0-590-43183-8
[1. Stars—Fiction. 2. Imaginary playmates—Fiction.
3. Alligators—Fiction.] I. Title.
PZ7.S87792Go 1990
[E]—dc20

89-33738
CIP
AC

12 11 10 9 8 7 6 5 4 3 2 1   0 1 2 3 4 5/9

Design by Tracy Arnold

Printed in the U.S.A.   36

First Scholastic printing, March 1990

Good Night
Twinklegator

by Kazuko G. Stone

Scholastic Inc. ◇ New York

It was a beautiful night. The gentle moon rose among the bright, glittery stars in the crisp night sky.

Aligay went to bed early. Looking up at the sky, he
began to play connect the dots with the twinkling stars.

He connected several gleaming stars to make an alligator.

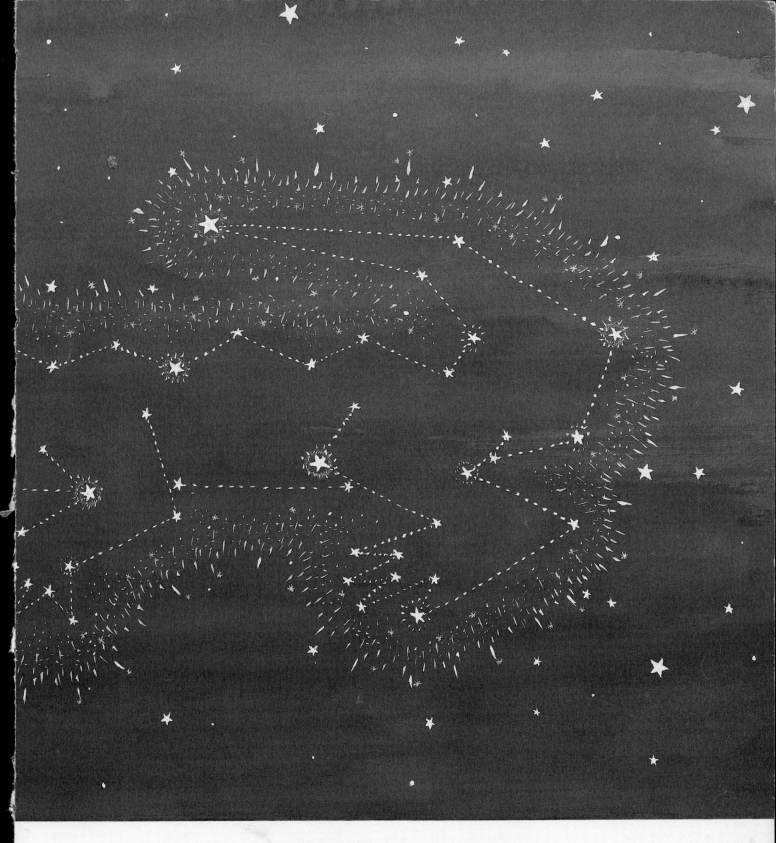

Aligay named him Twinklegator
because he twinkled so brightly.

Twinklegator got very hungry up in the sky, so he glided toward the moon to take a taste. To Twinklegator, the moon looked like a delicious, golden pancake.

"Don't eat the moon!" called Aligay.
"The moon is my friend!"

"But I'm hungry," cried Twinklegator.
"Wait," said Aligay. "I'll make you some food."

Aligay made a pancake, a fish, some bananas, a watermelon slice, and all sorts of good things.

"Thank you. That was delicious," Twinklegator said happily.
"Now I'm full. But I'm not very sleepy yet."

And he flew down like a shooting star.

"Good evening, Twinklegator," said Aligay.

"Good evening, Aligay," he said when he reached the ground.
"Let's take a walk."

In the jungle, everybody was sleeping peacefully. The monkeys were asleep in their beds in the trees. The birds were asleep high in their nests.

Aligay and Twinklegator tiptoed by, very, very quietly.
Shhhhh...

Soon they came to a field. In the grass they found a butterfly,
a grasshopper, and a ladybug. They were all sleeping on
hammocks, swinging in the breeze.

They found a spider sleeping in a soft, silky net, and a dragonfly sleeping on some bent, brown grass. Shhhhh...

"Let's go swimming," Aligay said, pointing to the pond.

So they ran across the moonlit field.

In the water, all the fish were sleeping silently in their seaweed beds.

Aligay and Twinklegator swam very, very quietly.
Shhhhh...

When they came out of the water, Twinklegator was very, very sleepy. He began to cry.

"What's the matter?" asked Aligay.
"Everyone has a bed to sleep in but me."

"Don't worry," said Aligay. "I'll make you a nice, comfortable hammock just like mine. Look up in the sky."

And Aligay connected the stars into a beautiful,
twinkling hammock.

"Thank you so very much! And good night, Aligay,"
Twinklegator said gratefully, and glided up to his bed.

"Good night, Twinklegator!"
And everyone went happily to sleep.

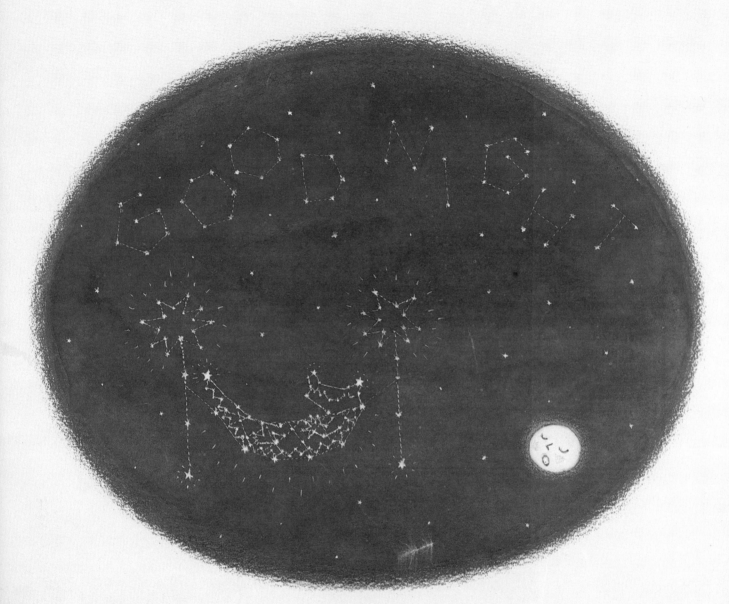

Shhhhh...